"For Isaac and Oscar - always treat life as one big mela."

\- Chitra Soundar

Farmer Falgu Goes to the Kumbh Mela

Chitra Soundar

Kanika Nair

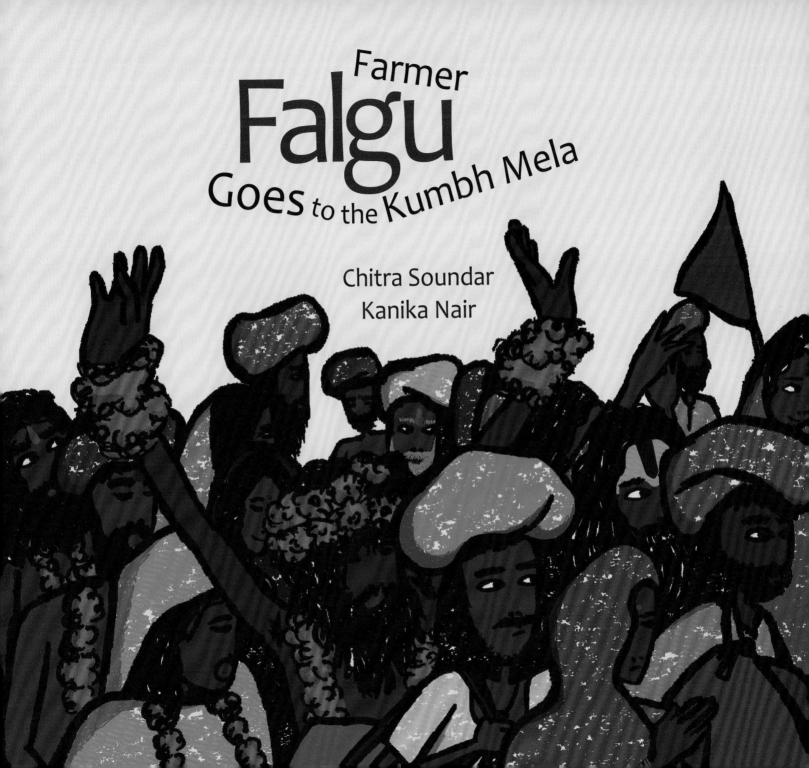

Farmer Falgu decided to go to Allahabad for the Kumbh Mela festival.

"Don't forget to try the delicious jalebis and the sweet lassi," said his wife.

Farmer Falgu nodded as he packed some clothes.

"Don't miss the procession of sadhus," reminded the temple priest.

"Don't forget to see the **elephants**," suggested the ticket checker.

DHADAK!

DHADAK!

rattled the train on the tracks.

Farmer Falgu fell asleep.

ALLAHABAD Jn.

इलाहाबाद जं.

Farmer Falgu woke up as the
train reached the station.

The platform was crowded.

He set off towards the sacred river.

Farmer Falgu reached the river and was waiting for the procession of sadhus, when an old woman asked for help.

"Sure, sure," he said, carrying her big bag towards the pilgrims' tents.

By the time Farmer Falgu returned, the procession had gone past, leaving behind just the echo of the cymbals.

CHALANG!

CHALANG!

He sighed.
"Maybe next time," he consoled himself.

While Farmer Falgu waited for the parade of elephants, a little girl tugged at his shirt.

"Help me," she cried.
"I am lost. I want my Ma!"

"Don't worry,"
said Farmer Falgu,
and went in search
of a policeman.

By the time Farmer Falgu returned, after reuniting mother and daughter, the elephants had turned the corner, leaving behind just the faint sound of their bells.

CLANG - CLANG!

"Not again!" he said. "I can't believe I missed the elephants too! Maybe next time."

Farmer Falgu headed towards
the riverbank for a dip.

DHADAM!

A man on crutches had slipped on the
muddy ground. Farmer Falgu helped
him up and took him to the first-aid tent.

Just as he was about to return to the river,
Farmer Falgu realized how late it was.

"Oh dear," he said. "Maybe next time.
I should leave now if I have to catch my train."

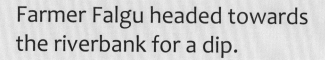

As Farmer Falgu made his way to the station, the smell of butter and sugar wafted from the stalls.

He stopped for a moment to sniff the air. "Maybe I can get some jalebis," he thought.

But the queue for the sweet shop was a mile long. There was simply no time.

When he reached the station, he found that the train was delayed by two hours.

"Maybe now is the time," he said, filled with hope. He rushed back to the river.

The riverside was not crowded. Farmer Falgu took a dip in the cold water three times.

CHALANG!

CHALANG!

He turned around in surprise. The procession of sadhus was making its way to the river.

CLANG - CLANG!

Farmer Falgu could not believe his luck. Behind the procession were the elephants ambling down the street.

He let out a happy cry.

He returned to the station just in time for his train.

Just as Farmer Falgu found a seat,
someone tapped him on the shoulder.

"Falgu! Here, have some jalebis!" said a familiar voice.
It was Kishan, Farmer Falgu's best friend! "Some lassi too,"
offered Kishan, smiling. "Perfect," said Farmer Falgu.

As the train chugged its way back home,
Farmer Falgu closed his eyes and smiled.

"How was the trip?" asked Farmer Falgu's wife, when he reached home.

"Unbelievable!"

he replied.

"I should have come too," she said.

"Surely next time,"
said Farmer Falgu.

About the Kumbh Mela

Kumbh Mela in Hindi means 'Festival of the Pot'. According to Hindu mythology, the Devas (demigods), fearing what would happen if the Asuras (demons) drank from the pot containing the Nectar of Immortality, stole the pot.

As the pot was being carried away to a safe hiding place, the nectar spilled at the banks of four rivers making these places sacred. These were Haridwar (river Ganges), Nashik (river Godavari), Ujjain (river Kshipra) and Allahabad (the confluence of rivers Ganga, Yamuna, and Saraswati).

Pilgrims arrive from all over India and the world to attend the Kumbh Mela. This spectacular event is held once in twelve years in any one of these four places.

Apart from the marvelous processions of the Sadhus (the holy men), and colorful scenes of jubilation and street food like jalebis (a sweet snack) and lassis (a yoghurt-based drink), the highlight of the festival is the holy dip that people take in the waters of the rivers.

CHITRA SOUNDAR

Chitra hails from India, resides in London and lives in imaginary worlds weaved
out of stories. She has written over twenty books for children aged 3 to 10 years.
Chitra also loves to retell folktales, legends, and ancient tales from the Indian
subcontinent. While she dabbles in chapter books, her first love is picture books.

KANIKA NAIR

Kanika Nair has always had a passion for illustration. After receiving a bachelor's
degree in Communication Design from Pearl Academy of Fashion, New Delhi, she
began working as a freelance illustrator, writer, and designer of children's books.
She loves to incorporate various insights about children that she has collected
over the years into her illustrations. The Indian cultural canvas has always
fascinated her and this is quite evident in her style of illustration.

Farmer Falgu Goes to the Kumbh Mela

Text copyright © 2017 Chitra Soundar.
Illustration copyright © 2017 Karadi Tales Company Pvt. Ltd.

First U.S. Print 2018

Text: Chitra Soundar
Illustrations: Kanika Nair

Karadi Tales Company Pvt. Ltd.
3A, Dev Regency, 11, First Main Road,
Gandhinagar, Adyar, Chennai 600 020
Tel: +91 44 4205 4243
email: contact@karaditales.com
Website: www.karaditales.com

Cataloging - in - Publication information:

Chitra Soundar
Farmer Falgu Goes to the Market / Chitra Soundar;
Illustrated by Kanika Nair
p.32; color illustrations; 23 x 20.5 cm.

JUV000000   JUVENILE FICTION / General
JUV030020   JUVENILE FICTION / People & Places / Asia
JUV033260   JUVENILE FICTION / Religious / Hindu
JUV039220   JUVENILE FICTION / Social Themes / Values & Virtues

ISBN 978-81-8190-355-6

Distributed in the United States by Consortium Book Sales & Distribution
www.cbsd.com